Vanish

Karen
Spafford-Fitz

Orca currents

ORCA BOOK PUBLISHERS

Library and Archives Canada Cataloguing in Publication

Spafford-Fitz, Karen, 1963-
Vanish / Karen Spafford-Fitz.
(Orca currents)

Issued also in electronic formats.
ISBN 978-1-4598-0355-8 (bound).--ISBN 978-1-4598-0349-7 (pbk.)

I. Title. II. Series: Orca currents
PS8637.P33V35 2013   jC813'.6   C2012-907299-0

First published in the United States, 2013
Library of Congress Control Number: 2012952474

Summary: Fourteen-year-old Simone is a key witness
in a parental abduction investigation.

*Orca Book Publishers is dedicated to preserving the environment and has
printed this book on Forest Stewardship Council® certified paper.*

Orca Book Publishers gratefully acknowledges the support for its
publishing programs provided by the following agencies: the Government
of Canada through the Canada Book Fund and the Canada Council for the Arts,
and the Province of British Columbia through the BC Arts Council
and the Book Publishing Tax Credit.

Cover photography by Getty Images

ORCA BOOK PUBLISHERS   ORCA BOOK PUBLISHERS
PO Box 5626, Stn. B   PO Box 468
Victoria, BC Canada   Custer, WA, USA
V8R 6S4   98240-0468

www.orcabook.com

Printed and bound in Canada.

16 15 14 13 • 4 3 2 1

To those who look out for their buddies
and especially to Ken, Anna and Shannon.

Chapter One

For the hundredth time, I wish I had never moved to this school. I especially wish I hadn't moved here five minutes before the school year started. That's how I ended up in this crappy class. Leadership studies was the only option class that had spaces left when I registered. Trust me, nothing else would make me take grade-eight leadership studies.

At my last school, the leadership study kids had to deliver speeches about bullying or school spirit to classes of bored students. Usually one kid in a presentation group does most of the talking. I have a quiet voice and a major phobia about speaking in front of other people. I plan to become an expert at making posters this year.

Right now, the leadership class is standing in the hall, waiting to start a Kinderbuddy program. We're going to be working with the kindergarten class.

"I'm stepping inside to help out," says Ms. Boyd. She gives our class a deadly glare. "And in case anyone feels like talking, I've got a big stack of caution cards." Her hand twitches toward her pocket.

If you get a caution card, you have to write out what you did, why you did it and your plan for avoiding that behavior in the future. You also have to do volunteer work around the school. Apparently, scrubbing the goop from kids' spaghetti lunches out of the school microwave is the best way to ponder your lapse of judgment.

I glance through the window into the kindergarten classroom. Little girls with pigtails and little boys in super-hero T-shirts scramble to put away storybooks.

Ms. Boyd is directing traffic. This might take awhile. And, unfortunately, I'm standing right beside the richest, most spoiled teenagers in the history of forever. Their names are Stacy, Miranda and Tessa, but I think of them as the Runway Girls. As usual, they are working through their three favorite topics of discussion.

The first topic is fashion. I buy all my clothes at the thrift store. These girls spend every weekend buying the latest styles at the mall. I bet even their underwear has designer labels. They were born with mascara wands and eyeliner pencils in their hands too.

The second topic is all the trips their rich mommies and daddies take them on. Maui, Malibu Beach and Mexico are at the top of their lists. This is another sore point for me. My dad took off before I was born. We haven't heard from him since. It's always been just Mom and me. Her jobs never pay well, and we're always struggling to make ends meet. Holidays are out of the question.

Their third favorite topic is guys. Apparently, no guy here in Edmonton compares to the celebrity look-alikes they see on their spectacular holidays. That doesn't stop the Runway Girls from constantly crushing on Aaron. As usual, they have squeezed in as close as possible to him.

Stacy bumps into me as she spins around. "I hate this top. I'm gonna ditch it when I get home."

"But it's totally cute on you," Tessa says. "You've gotta wear it again. Please?"

I roll my eyes. Why does it matter to Tessa if Stacy wears that shirt again?

"It is seriously cute," Miranda says. "Don't you think so, Aaron?"

I take in Aaron's messy brown hair and the gray skulls on his black hoodie. He shrugs, then looks away. Strange. At my last school, the guys practically beat their chests with excitement when the popular girls talked to them. But Aaron seems baffled by the attention of the Runway Girls.

"Ooh, look at Simone." Stacy points a manicured finger at me. "She's checking Aaron out."

My face burns and my throat clenches. It would be nice to have some friends to hide behind. But I haven't made any friends here. Everyone at my old school seems to have forgotten about me too. None of my so-called friends from my last school has messaged me on Facebook for months. For all they care, I might as well vanish into thin air.

Ms. Boyd steps into the hall and clears her throat. "We're heading into the kindergarten class in one minute."

Fake squeals of glee drift forward. Ms. Boyd's hand flits toward her over-stuffed caution-card pocket.

"Keep this up, and some of you will miss the pizza lunch on Friday."

Ms. Boyd delivers one more menacing glare before she disappears back into the kindergarten room.

"She can't do that." Stacy pouts. "It's none of her business what we eat for lunch."

Tessa pouts too. "Anyway, this Kinderbuddy project sucks."

"Yeah." Miranda swishes her blond hair. "If Ms. Boyd is so desperate to work with little kids, she should teach kindergarten instead of grade eight."

"Can you imagine her teaching kindergarten?" Stacy laughs. "She'd terrorize them."

"Yeah," Miranda says. "She'd have the little ankle-biters peeing themselves."

"Ahem." Ms. Boyd thrusts three caution cards at the Runway Girls.

Their mouths fall open in surprise. I duck my head so they won't see the huge smile on my face.

Chapter Two

The kindergarten kids are sitting in the middle of the carpet. Ms. Boyd has a demented warning look in her eye as she arranges us around them. Then she signals to the kindergarten teacher to begin.

"Welcome to the kindergarten classroom, grade eights. My name is Mrs. Mankowski. I am delighted to have you here. We are going to work in buddies throughout the school year. We'll be doing artwork and reading projects. We will also be planning a Halloween party together. After Christmas, the kindergarten students will need help with the Valentine's Day party. Later, there's the Mother's Day brunch to organize."

Two wiggly little boys are bouncing on the carpet. Ms. Boyd takes the arm of the wiggliest boy. She points for him to move to the other side of the carpet.

He drops down beside a little girl who looks like she just stepped out of a Barbie-doll box. Barbie Girl has a blond braid. She is wearing a pink fluffy sweater and pink tights. I wonder if this is how the Runway Girls looked when they were in kindergarten.

Barbie Girl notices all the grade eights watching her. She looks down and fixes her eyes on her pink ballet slippers.

She looks like she wants to disappear. In that shy moment, my heart lurches. I know exactly how that feels. I decide I like her despite the Barbie look.

"I am going to start assigning you to your buddies," Mrs. Mankowski continues. "And remember, one of the goals of the Kinderbuddy project is for you to learn to work with new people. That means there will be no switching partners."

Mrs. Mankowski starts calling out names of Big Buddies and Kinder-buddies. The buddies sit together on the carpet or at a table. More than half the kids have been paired up.

"Simone Marchant?"

I raise my hand slightly.

"Simone and Yuri."

I look around for my Kinderbuddy. Nobody answers. The little boy who got moved earlier is doing backflips on the carpet.

"Yuri," Mrs. Mankowski says, "no somersaults in the classroom."

This is my Kinderbuddy?

I can feel the horrified look on my face. The leadership kids start laughing.

Yuri is still not joining me, so I go to him. Barbie Girl shifts over for me to sit between them. Yuri nearly kicks me in the head as I sink down onto the carpet.

Mrs. Mankowski continues. "Now for the last two students, Lily"—Barbie Girl looks up—"and Aaron McGavin."

"A *boy* buddy?" Lily's lower lip quivers. "But I want a *girl* buddy."

Mrs. Mankowski shakes her head. "You have to work with the Big Buddy you were assigned. Just like everyone else."

Lily's enormous brown eyes are filling with tears.

"Lily," Mrs. Mankowski says, "I taught Aaron when he was in kindergarten. He is a very nice boy."

The Runway Girls start nudging each other.

"I think he's a very nice boy too," Tessa says.

Stacy nods and smiles widely, her eyes fixed on Aaron. But Aaron is not having the same effect on Lily. Her eyes are darting between Aaron's face and the skulls on his hoodie. Her lips tremble.

"I want this *girl* Big Buddy." Lily clutches me and starts to sob. "Not that boy."

I wait until Lily pauses. Then I turn toward Mrs. Mankowski.

"How about a trade?" I ask. "I'd really like to be Kinderbuddies with Lily. That is, if Yuri doesn't mind."

Yuri scampers across the room. He grabs the doorknob with two hands and walks his legs up the door. With a leg on either side of the doorknob and his head brushing the floor, he looks like a baby orangutan.

"I don't know." Mrs. Mankowski's eyes flit toward Ms. Boyd. "I can't have students changing partners."

I think fast. I need to trade buddies without Mrs. Mankowski losing face in front of Ms. Boyd.

"Someone shut that kid up," Tessa mutters behind me.

I can't believe how mean she is! But at least I'm angry enough to speak louder than my usual whisper.

"We don't have to change partners for good," I say. "But could the four of us—me and Lily, and Aaron and Yuri—work in a group today? That might help Lily get to know Aaron better."

Lily does not look sure about this. Clearly, she would rather not work with Aaron at all.

Mrs. Mankowski nods her head. I turn to Lily.

"I'm Simone," I tell her. "We get to work together. But we need to work with Aaron and Yuri too. Right?"

Lily gives me a teary smile and nods.

With Lily glued to me, I step toward Aaron. Yuri stops his orangutan routine and bounces over. Then he grabs the bottom of Aaron's hoodie and stuffs his head up underneath it.

Aaron tries to pull away, but Yuri has a tight grip. Finally, Aaron unzips his hoodie and hands it to Yuri. "Here, you can wear it for now. But you have to give it back later."

Ms. Boyd can't stand any more delays. "Mrs. Mankowski, please explain what the students will do today."

Mrs. Mankowski nods. "For the past few weeks, the kindergarten kids have been talking about what they might like to be when they grow up.

"Today, I will give each Kinderbuddy a large sheet of paper to lie down on. The Big Buddies will trace around them. Then together you can draw in the special clothing and the special equipment required for the Kinderbuddy's job. For example, if the Kinderbuddy wants to be a firefighter, you could draw a fire hose. If the Kinderbuddy wants to be a chef, you might draw a baker's hat and apron. The Big Buddies will cut the pictures out. Then you can color them together."

The Kinderbuddies dash toward a stack of oversized paper. Seconds later, Yuri zips back to the carpet, his paper flapping around him. Lily hands me her paper and practically sits on my lap. She is making it clear that she is working with me instead of Aaron. It has been a long time since anyone chose me for anything. So even though Lily is just in kindergarten, it feels nice that she picked me to be her buddy.

Aaron takes the paper from Yuri. "What do you want to be when you grow up?"

"Two things." Yuri is spinning in circles. "A police officer and a monster."

Aaron and I burst out laughing. The Runway Girls shoot jealous looks at me.

"Think about it some more, Yuri, while I trace you."

As Aaron tries to coax Yuri to lie still, I turn to Lily. "What do you want to be when you grow up?"

"A vet and a ballerina."

"Both at the same time?"

"Yes." Lily's eyes grow even bigger.

"Okay," I say. "We can draw you wearing a ballerina's skirt with a veterinarian's jacket over top."

Lily nods. "But the ballerina skirt has to show through. And I need a kitty cat and a puppy too."

Lily lies down on the paper, and I trace around her.

Aaron has way more trouble. "Yuri, you need to take my hoodie off so I can trace you."

Yuri pulls the hood tightly over his face. "Look! I'm an alien!"

"Yeah, I believe you," Aaron says. "Just take the hoodie off for now."

Yuri pulls off the hoodie and flings it onto the floor. Then he flings himself onto the paper.

"Stop wiggling while I count to ten," Aaron says, "or I'll stuff you in my locker."

Yuri thinks this is a great idea. He pesters Aaron to stuff him in the locker right now.

Aaron holds Yuri down while I trace around him. He is wiggling so much that I mostly draw him freehand.

Aaron hands the hoodie back to Yuri. He's great with little kids. It's too bad he didn't realize that a hoodie with skulls might terrify a little pink Kinderbuddy.

When I finally look up again, I notice that the Runway Girls look miserable. Stacy is mopping up glue that her Kinderbuddy spilled across her expensive jeans. Miranda is shaking out the pencil shavings that her Kinderbuddy spilled into her fancy tote bag. Tessa looks bored.

Lily is drawing puppies and kittens. She giggles as she glues them onto the pockets of her veterinary coat. A pink tutu shows through the open coat.

I am cutting out a puppy when someone bangs into me.

"Lily, honey! Are you all right today?" The woman drapes herself around Lily. "Mommy thought you might need to see her before home time."

Really? Lily was fine before her mom arrived. But now even the grade eights are watching. Lily shrinks like she did earlier.

"Ms. Warnicke," Mrs. Mankowski says, "can we chat over by my desk?"

Lily's mom hugs her daughter, then joins the teacher.

"Do you need to leave early today?" I ask. "Is that why your mom is here?"

Lily shakes her head. Then she speaks so softly, I can hardly hear her. "Sometimes Mommy checks on me. To see I'm okay."

Ms. Warnicke is still chatting with Lily's teacher. Her eyes are on me the whole time. Jeez, does she think I'm going to take off with her daughter or something?

Ms. Boyd steps to the front of the class a few minutes later. "Time to go, grade eights."

"Bye, Lily. I'll see you next time."

Lily waves as I leave the kindergarten class with the leadership group. I smile and wave back. Her mom is still talking to Mrs. Mankowski. I don't get what that was all about.

Then I step into the hallway and I realize it's happened. For the first time, I have actually enjoyed myself at Cherney Gates School.

Chapter Three

"Curriculum Night is coming up in a few weeks." Those are the first words out of Ms. Boyd's mouth at our next leadership class. I imagine all the presentations Ms. Boyd will make us do. That thought makes me cringe.

"We have a lot to do before then, but I also need some volunteers to go back to the kindergarten class today.

Some of you did not make much progress last class with the Kinderbuddy career pictures." Ms. Boyd picks out a few kids, including the Runway Girls, with her killer glare. "I told Mrs. Mankowski I would send her some helpers this afternoon."

My hand flies into the air on its own.

"Simone and…" Ms. Boyd looks around the class.

Normally some friends would volunteer as a group. But that's not going to happen in my case.

Eventually Fiona raises her hand. Fiona is not a Runway Girl, but she looks like she's waiting for the perfect moment to rush into their glamorous world.

Ms. Boyd then "volunteers" two other kids—Luka and Davis. We are about to leave the classroom when Aaron's hand shoots up. I notice the Runway Girls have edged their desks closer to him. "Do you need anyone else?" he asks.

Ms. Boyd nods. "Actually, I could use one more volunteer."

I'm not surprised when the Runway Girls start coaxing Ms. Boyd to let them go too.

"Come on, Ms. Boyd," Miranda says. "I really want to work with Brendan today."

"How fascinating," Ms. Boyd says in a dry tone. "Especially since your Kinderbuddy is named Braden. Not Brendan. Now sit down and forget about leaving this class."

When we get to the kindergarten room, I take Lily's picture from the pile first. Yuri sees Aaron, and he tumbles over too. The four of us work in the same spot as last time.

Lily and I finish coloring her veterinary coat. Aaron tries to help Yuri decide on his career choice. Yuri still cannot get past the idea of being a monster.

"How about a police officer?" Aaron says. "You'd be really good at it."

"Okay, okay. But only if you draw me with seventeen guns. And a big stick for smacking bad guys."

"Okay," Aaron says. "But you'll have to be extra sneaky to fool the bad guys. We'll hide the guns in secret pockets on your uniform."

Yuri actually slows down long enough to help draw.

Now that we have finished Lily's picture, she is checking out my necklace.

"I like this." She touches each bead.

"Thanks. I made it last week."

"Really?"

I nod. "My mom used to make jewelry. She taught me how."

"Could you make one for me too?" Then Lily covers her mouth with her hands. "Oops! It's not polite to ask."

"That's okay. I love making neck-laces. I could make you one and bring it next class."

Lily's eyes light up. "Do you know how to make rings too?"

"No. Only beaded necklaces and bracelets," I say. "Do you want me to use pink beads for your necklace?"

Lily shakes her head. "No. My mom always gets me pink things. But I'll tell you my *real* favorite color." She leans over and whispers into my ear. "Green."

"Really? Are you saying that because my necklace is green?"

Lily shakes her head.

"Okay," I say. "I have lots more green beads. I'll bring your necklace next class."

Lily gives me a cute little-kid hug. Unfortunately, it attracts Mrs. Mankowski's attention. "Now that you have finished, Lily, you need to pick a new activity. Simone needs to help some of the other Kinderbuddies."

Lily reluctantly walks over to the paint center. I'm sure it is no accident that I am working right beside it.

For the rest of the class, I help cut out nurses' uniforms, hockey sticks, fishing rods, and garbage pails for the trash collectors. I have barely finished when the kids start getting ready to go home. It takes them ages to tie their shoes and zip up their jackets. I had no idea home time was such a big production for kindergarten kids.

Lily breaks away from the group. "Simone, can you play with me outside after school?"

"Okay. Once I'm done at my locker."

Lily gives me a quick hug. "I'll be at the pirate ship!"

Later, as I'm walking toward the playground, I hear "*Simone*! *Simone*!"

The Runway Girls are cutting across the schoolyard. They imitate Lily calling me. I drop my backpack at my feet and pretend I'm looking for something inside. It's clear to the world that I'm not as cool as the Runway Girls. I'm not even sure that I want to be. But still, I wait for them to leave.

Thank goodness they are too cool to hang around for long. Once they are out of sight, I join Lily and her friends on the wooden pirate ship. We have a good hard stomp on the gangplank. Their moms eventually collect them and herd them into their vans to go home.

Chapter Four

Mrs. Mankowski pulls me aside the next time the leadership class is in the kindergarten room. "Simone, would you consider leaving your last class ten minutes early each day? I could use some help getting the kindergarten students ready for dismissal. It's a big job, especially when they'll need snowsuits and boots and mittens in another month."

I am about to say yes when Mrs. Mankowski's smile vanishes. I turn. Ms. Boyd is standing behind me.

"I'm not sure that's a good idea," Ms. Boyd says. "Simone could use that time at the end of the day to meet more kids her own age."

I feel like Ms. Boyd has kicked me in the stomach. Sure, what she said is true. But I like helping the Kinderbuddies. It gives me something to do other than feel awkward around the Runway Girls and their friends. I try to think of something to say. The only thing that pops into my head is a complete lie.

"Actually, I have tons of friends at my old school. We message each other all the time."

Ms. Boyd stares straight into my face for what feels like an hour. I try not to think about the real story. About how I checked Facebook again last night and my so-called friends still hadn't messaged me.

I can't tell if Ms. Boyd believes me or not. She finally nods. "Then if Simone would like to help, I am fine with that."

Mrs. Mankowski smiles. "Thanks, Simone. That will be great."

Lily, meanwhile, is practically waving her hand off trying to get my attention. I couldn't possibly miss her pink-flowered dress and matching hair band and tights.

Lily and I go to our usual place. Yuri rolls across the carpet to join us. I notice the jealous looks from the Runway Girls as Aaron sits down beside me.

I reach into my pocket and take out the necklace I made for Lily.

"Oh, Simone! It's exactly like yours!" Lily is wide-eyed.

"Yes. Except yours is Kinderbuddy-sized."

Lily hugs me. "I knew you wouldn't forget. I brought something for you too." She pulls a paper from the pocket of her dress and unfolds it. It is a picture she has drawn of kittens and puppies.

At that moment, Mrs. Mankowski starts to talk.

"I have something else for you too," Lily whispers. "I'll give it to you later."

"Today, the Kinderbuddies need help with another important job," Mrs. Mankowski says. "We have talked about how knowing their phone numbers and addresses can help keep them safe. Most of them know their phone numbers already. So today, the Big Buddies need to help them learn their addresses.

"I have written each Kinderbuddy's name and address on a slip of paper. When the Kinderbuddies can correctly say their address three times, they can come get a card and an envelope. The Kinderbuddy's job is to decorate the front of the card. The Big Buddy's job is to print a message inside the card and print the address on the envelope. I will put stamps on the envelopes and take them to the post office. The Kinderbuddies will soon get their special letters in the mail."

This is almost more excitement than Yuri can stand. He is hopping like a frog as he calls out numbers.

"What did you say?" Aaron asks.

Mrs. Mankowski walks by. "Yuri already knows his phone number and address. He might get a little bored this period." She smiles. "Good luck."

Aaron unrolls the slip of paper that Yuri is clutching. "Say your address for me again, Yuri."

Yuri shouts out a string of numbers.

"Yuri, you're a star! Go get the card and envelope."

Lily is having a harder time. "The numbers are confusing."

"I know," I say. "It's hard because your address only has numbers in it. Do you know what the different numbers look like?"

"Most of them."

"Okay. Let's read them together."

Lily reads the numbers with me. But she mixes them up when she is not looking at the paper.

"I don't remember those numbers from my house," she says.

"I'll check that Mrs. Mankowski wrote the right numbers on the paper. Maybe she made a mistake."

Lily looks longingly at the card that Aaron and Yuri are drawing. Mrs. Mankowski pulls out a binder that says *Emergency Contact Info*.

"What did I write down for Lily?"

"One-one-four-zero-nine Seventy-First A Avenue."

"Yes, that's the correct address," Mrs. Mankowski says. "Lily needs to practice more."

Lily plops down on the carpet. Suddenly her face lights up. "Remember I brought something else for you?"

She reaches into the pocket of her dress. "I know you make necklaces and bracelets. And I want you to have a pretty ring too."

The ring that Lily drops into my hand is all bent and scratched. I smile and slip it on my finger.

"Thanks, Lily. I love it. And I'll keep my hand right here so I can look at it while we practice your address."

Yuri and Aaron have almost finished Yuri's card.

"You're great with numbers," Aaron says. "You should get a cell phone. You won't even have to program your friends' numbers into it."

"Okay. I'll ask my mom for one tonight," says Yuri.

"She might think you're a bit young," I say. "I don't even have a cell phone yet." I don't mention that I'll probably never get one. I'm sure it would cost too much money.

"Do you have a cell phone, Aaron?" Yuri is wide-eyed.

Aaron nods.

"Teach me your cell-phone number. I can phone you later."

Aaron hesitates, but he eventually gives in.

I listen as Aaron tells Yuri his cell-phone number. I'm pretty good with numbers too. Aaron's cell number is soon dancing through my head. Not that I will ever actually phone him.

Lily's lips move as she practices the last few numbers of her address. "There! I did it!"

"You know the whole thing?" I ask.

"Pretty sure."

"You have to say it three times exactly right," I say.

The first time, Lily gets everything right except for the last number. She gets it perfectly after that. I tuck the slip of paper into my pocket as she gets the card and the envelope.

"Do you like your ring, Simone?"

"Yes. It's really pretty. Where did you get it?"

"It's been at my house for a long time. I use it for playing dress-up."

"Are you sure you won't miss it?"

"Nope." Lily's mind jumps to something else. "Can you play after school today?"

"Of course," I say. "Remember I told you I would?"

Lily nods. She always asks me over and over. I guess that's a little-kid thing.

I have fun playing Eagle's Eye and Red Rover with the Kinderbuddies after school. Lots of their moms stand around and chat while we play. Some of them have even asked for my phone number so they can call me to babysit. Nobody has phoned me yet, but I think it's going to happen sometime.

The moms are nice, but Lily's mom is hard to get to know. And she's the one I see the most. She often shows up at Lily's class when I'm helping the Kinderbuddies get ready to go home. I can't figure her out. Last week, she was really nice. She told me to call her Rachel instead of Ms. Warnicke. But every day since then, she has ignored me. Some days she acts so angry that I wonder if I offended her and need to apologize for something.

We are playing tag when Lily spots her mom. As usual, Lily does not call out hi.

Instead, she says, "Mom, Simone needs to babysit me sometime soon."

"You go play now, Lily. Simone and I can talk about that."

Wide-eyed with hope, Lily scampers off. "You know, Simone," Rachel says, "I'd love to have you babysit, but I don't often leave Lily. It's been hard for her since her father and I divorced. She needs to know I'm near at hand."

Rachel looks closely at me. It's like she's measuring my reaction carefully.

I don't know what to say, so I just nod. Thankfully, Lily calls me. I go sit on top of the monkey bars with her.

"Almost time to go home," Rachel calls.

"But there's no school tomorrow. I won't see Simone for a whole weekend."

"Five minutes more," Rachel says. "That's all."

We dangle from the monkey bars, bounce on the walkway and play at being pirate-ship queens before Lily leaves with her mom. As they drive away in their van, the last thing I see is Lily's face pressed against the glass. She is waving madly at me. I wave madly back at her, then start walking home.

Chapter Five

I sit down at the computer once I get home from school. There's probably no point in checking Facebook, but I log on anyway. Maybe this is the day that Danielle and Lauren will have messaged me.

Once again, there's nothing. Not a single message from either of them. My whole body goes limp. I don't want to believe they don't care about me, but it sure looks that way.

I scroll through my message history. It's like I thought. I sent the last three messages to Danielle and the last four messages to Lauren. But I haven't heard back from either of them. Tears burn my eyes as I make my decision. I am not going to message them again until they send me a message back. If they ever do.

Just then, I hear the front door open.

"Hi, Simone."

"Mom, you're home!" I wipe my eyes quickly.

"Don't sound so shocked." Mom smiles as she appears in the doorway.

"Well, you've been working a lot lately."

"I know. I've missed seeing you after school. These oddball shifts are getting to me. Hopefully, I'll get more regular hours soon."

Neither of us says a word, but we're probably thinking the same thing. That this job at the deli isn't what Mom wants at all. It's the only job she could find after the jewelry store shut down. That job didn't pay much either, but at least Mom liked working there.

"It's okay though," Mom says. "Somehow things always work out. This will too."

I don't answer.

"Like with this house," Mom continues. "This fell into our laps, right? I love that we're finally living in a nice house in a nice neighborhood."

We got this house because the Evans family needed someone to house-sit while they are working overseas this year. Mom seems so happy that I don't mention how we'll have to move again when they return from Saudi Arabia.

"And think about how everything is going so great at your new school."

I swallow hard. I'm extra glad I didn't tell Mom about not making any friends yet.

"Come on." Mom motions for me to follow her into the kitchen. "So what happened at school today?"

Mom pulls a pizza crust and toppings out of a grocery bag. While we put pepperoni and cheese on the pizza, I tell her about the Kinderbuddies. "The moms even want me to babysit for them sometime. That would help bring in extra money, right?"

Mom looks serious again. "You are way too young to have to worry about that."

I don't want to get into that now. Instead, I tell Mom about the life-sized ballerina-vet picture and about teaching Lily her address. I reach into my backpack and pull out a stack of pictures. I pass them to Mom.

"Did Lily make all of these?"

I nod. "She's constantly drawing me pictures."

Mom smiles as she flips through them. Most of the pictures have hearts and balloons and ponies on them. And they all say the same thing at the bottom. *Hi Simone. I love you. From Lily.*

"You could wallpaper your bedroom with these," Mom says.

"I know. I already taped some up in my locker too. Oh, and I made Lily a beaded necklace earlier this week. She gave me this ring." I hold out my hand.

"Can you take it off for me?" Mom asks.

She examines the inside edge. "Simone, this is real gold. It looks like a wedding band."

"It can't be. Look at all the scratches. It's bent too."

"Gold is quite soft. It scratches easily." Mom peers inside the ring again. "This is fourteen-karat gold."

"Seriously?"

Mom nods. "Look. It says so right here."

I have to squint to read the markings. Sure enough, it says *14 K*.

"I'll run it over to Lily's house first thing in the morning."

"Good idea," Mom says. "I think it can wait until then. Especially since we have a delicious pizza dinner to enjoy tonight."

The whole time I'm eating my pizza, I'm looking at that ring. I keep wondering where Lily got it. Or who she got it from.

Those thoughts distract me enough that I nearly forget—at least for now—about Danielle and Lauren having forgotten all about me.

Chapter Six

I can tell the house is empty when I wake up the next morning. Mom must have left early to open the deli.

It's almost noon by the time I finish breakfast. I'd planned to go to Lily's house earlier than this. Then I remember seeing a bike in the shed. Riding would be faster than walking.

I pull the bike out. The tires are a bit soft. I can't find a pump, so they will have to do. At least the helmet almost fits me.

As I take off down the driveway, I think of Lily mixing up the numbers in her address. Right now, I am thankful that the streets and avenues all have numbers. They make it easier to find your way around the city.

I turn onto Lily's avenue, and I soon find her house number. I take in the massive gardens and the big, sprawling house. I wonder what it would feel like to live in a beautiful house all the time. I wonder where we might live next. I shudder as I remember some of the tough neighborhoods we've lived in. The ones where you keep your head down and you walk really fast until you're safely inside your apartment.

I push those thoughts from my head as I ring the doorbell. Right away, I see an older man on the other side of the glass door. Lily's grandfather?

I smile, but the man does not smile back. But then, Rachel doesn't smile much either. Maybe that's how they are in her family.

"Hello," I say. "I have something to return to Lily."

"Which one is that? The woman or the little kid?"

"Lily is the little girl. She, uh, lives here."

The man shakes his head. "No, miss. She does not live here. But for some reason, that mother of hers tells everyone that they do."

I'm too confused to say anything. The man's expression softens. Instead of looking angry, he looks grumpy. I think that is an improvement.

"I chatted with that woman for ten minutes last summer while I was out gardening," he says. "Next thing I knew, she was giving out this address and coming by to pick up her mail. I should be charging her for every piece of mail I've taken in for her."

This doesn't make any sense. "Do you know where they really live?"

The man grumbles some more, then limps off down the hall. When he limps back, he is holding a piece of paper. "That woman—the mother—gave this to me about a month ago. She had the nerve to ask me to forward a parcel she was waiting for." He thrusts the paper into my hand. "Since you're going to see her, take this with you. And tell her I'm done forwarding her mail."

I take the paper. "Thank you, Mr.—"

"Cormigan. Charlie Cormigan."

"Thanks. I'll tell her."

Before I pedal away, I take another look at the address on the paper. Something about it sounds familiar. Where have I heard those numbers before?

It hits me once I get pedaling again. Those are the numbers Lily kept saying when we practiced her address. That explains why Lily was so confused. The numbers I was teaching her don't match the numbers she sees on her house every day. Now I am furious. The address I taught her won't help her if she ever gets lost.

Again I count street numbers and avenues. I am getting close to Lily's street. With their crooked porches and peeling paint and cracked windowpanes, many of these houses look as rough as the ones that Mom and I have lived in over the years.

"Watch out!"

I brake hard. Even still, I nearly hit the little dog that has bolted into the road. Then I realize I'm looking at a familiar face.

Aaron reaches down and picks up the dog. Two little boys are staring at us from the front yard.

"Sorry about that," Aaron says. "Kermit just slipped out of the house."

"Kermit?"

"Yeah. And that sure isn't the name I would have chosen."

The little boys tumble down the front yard, their arms outstretched.

"Take him straight into the house," Aaron says.

As they walk up the driveway, the taller boy holds Kermit tightly.

"Must be one of Aaron's girlfriends," the smaller boy says.

"Yeah," says the other, "One of those who keeps phoning."

My face burns as Aaron and I pretend we didn't hear. I'd bet a thousand bucks they were talking about the Runway Girls.

"Are those your brothers?" I ask.

Aaron nods.

"Oh. So that's how you know so much about working with little kids."

Aaron looks confused. "Oh. You mean with Yuri." Loud voices and laughter echo from inside the house. "Yeah, I guess. I've got one more little brother inside too."

"Wow. It's just me and my mom at my place."

"Sounds quiet," Aaron says with a laugh.

I nod. "Sometimes it's too quiet. Mom works a lot of funny hours."

Neither of us says anything for a few seconds.

"So you're out for a bike ride?" Aaron asks.

"Yeah. I'm riding to Lily's place." I hold out my hand. "She gave me this ring. I thought it was costume jewelry, but it's real, like, a wedding ring."

"Really?"

Aaron holds my hand to look at it. I feel myself blushing. I've got the ring on my left hand, too, like a real wedding ring. How stupid must that look?

Aaron shrugs. "It just looks like, I don't know, like a ring to me."

"Me too," I say. "But my mom knows a lot about jewelry. She says it's the real thing. Lily probably didn't know it was valuable. I'm heading to her house to give it back."

Aaron looks confused. "I heard her address when you were practicing in class. Isn't it over on Seventy-First A Avenue?"

I pull the slip of paper out of my pocket and look at it again. "Yeah, but that wasn't Lily's real address." I tell

Aaron what Mr. Cormigan said. "So I spent all that time teaching Lily the wrong address. She actually lives three blocks away from here."

"Aaron!" One of his brothers is calling from the front door. "It's your girlfriends on the phone!"

Aaron looks over his shoulder. "Tell them I'm not here."

"Too late. I already said you were out in the front yard," he says, "talking to another girlfriend."

If I were braver, I would say that I'm not another girlfriend. But it hits me that nobody asked Aaron if he wants to be the class heartthrob. I always assumed guys enjoy being adored by junior high girls. Maybe I'm wrong about that. Especially when the girls are super pushy, like the Runway Girls are.

"Guess I need to go," Aaron says. "See ya."

I hear the noise bursting from Aaron's house until I turn the corner. What would it be like living in the loudest house in the neighborhood?

It sounds like fun.

Chapter Seven

I know immediately that I have the right address this time. Lily's mom is outside by her van.

I have hardly stepped off my bike when Lily rushes out of the house. "Simone! Simone!"

I set the bike down as Lily throws herself at me, wrapping her arms tightly around my waist. I glance at Lily's mom. It's hard to tell what kind of mood Rachel is in today. Happy?

I take one more glance. No, definitely not happy. I had better keep this short.

I pull the ring from my finger and hold it out. "Lily gave this to me yesterday. I didn't know until last night that it's a real ring. Like, maybe a wedding ring. I brought it back as soon as I could."

Lily swallows hard. I hope I'm not getting her in trouble.

"Remember, Mommy, when you said you didn't like it? That you wished you never even saw it? That's why I gave it to Simone."

Rachel smiles, and her anger dissolves. "Thank you for returning this, Simone. And I'm sorry you caught us in such disarray. If there was a choice, we wouldn't be living here."

"Yeah," Lily pipes up. "But soon, we will have a pretty new house. Won't we, Mommy?"

My heart sinks. "You're moving?"

Lily nods. "Yes. To a pretty new house with flowers and a swing set. And we'll have dolphins to swim with," Lily continues, "and sand castles to build and waves to jump in."

"Don't worry," Rachel says. "Lily likes to talk that way sometimes." She turns back toward Lily. "We have fun dreaming about those things, don't we?"

Rachel's eyes land on the ring again. "Thanks again for returning this, Simone. You're right about it being my wedding ring. Lily must have found it in my dresser."

Rachel smiles at Lily. "Why don't you go get a juice box? You can get one for Simone too."

Lily grabs my hand and pulls me toward the house. Through the front window, I see boxes and suitcases with clothing and paper spilling out of them. There's an overflowing box of pink clothing. It's probably stuff that Lily has outgrown. Maybe they're collecting things for a garage sale.

We're about to step inside when Rachel calls out, "Lily, you go ahead. I'd like to chat with Simone for a moment."

It occurs to me that maybe Rachel is embarrassed about their messy house. I want to tell her that Mom and I have lived in way crappier places. That might make things worse, though, so I don't say anything.

"You probably had a hard time finding us," Rachel says.

"Mr. Cormigan gave me your address. I showed up there first. By mistake."

"I thought that might have been the case." She motions toward their house. "The truth is, this house is the best I can do. Lily's dad usually misses his child-support payments. But somehow Blake still finds time to swing by and harass me. That's why I've been using a false address—to keep Blake at arm's length."

Slowly the pieces start fitting together. The fake address, Rachel's mood swings, her visits to the school. I feel bad for wondering about her. What Rachel says next makes me feel even worse.

"It's been months since Lily had any contact with Blake. The last time was back in July."

"So he hasn't even talked to Lily in over three months?"

"I'm afraid not."

Given my father's disappearing act, I don't have a great opinion of dads to start with. Anger spreads like a massive heat wave across my face. It nearly chokes me.

"I should be used to it by now," Rachel says, "but it's been a hard day. I'm glad I didn't tell Lily that her dad was supposed to meet her at the park this morning."

Just then Lily bursts out of the kitchen door. She has two juice boxes in her hands and a big smile across her face. Even though she doesn't know her dad bailed on her today, I decide to make this a fun day for her anyway.

For the next two hours, we pile leaves and fling them into the air. We play Hula-Hoop and hopscotch. We sing Lily's favorite songs, and we dance across the yard. By the time I leave, I have done my best to make up for my little buddy's deadbeat dad.

Chapter Eight

I'm definitely getting better at managing leadership class. It's Curriculum Night, and I avoided the jobs that involve public speaking. In fact, I landed a great job—setting up a day care in the band room. Parents can leave their younger kids here so they can listen to the teachers without getting interrupted. I volunteered to do this as soon as

Ms. Boyd mentioned it. Fiona signed up to work in the day care too.

Fiona and I collected the art supplies, hauled stacks of library books into the room and pitched Fiona's tent for the kids to play in. We also have a Twister game and a sand table. The band teacher wasn't happy about the sand table. He told us we would have to vacuum the whole room for hours if anyone tipped sand on to the carpet. We promised to patrol that center extra closely.

Ms. Boyd passes through for an inspection. She doesn't actually praise us, but I've learned it's good when she doesn't say anything. I have almost forgiven her for telling Mrs. Mankowski that I need to make friends with kids my own age. I'm still not making any headway on that. I mostly don't think about it though.

Kids have started trickling into the room. Fiona and I move from one center to the next, showing them what to do. Then we tidy the center when a group leaves. I keep expecting Fiona to ditch me and take off after the Runway Girls. But so far, she hasn't. That surprises me.

I'm not surprised that Lily has already found me. As usual, she is sticking as closely as possible to me. We draw about a dozen pictures at the easel. She insists they are all for me. She writes her usual message at the bottom of each. *Hi Simone. I love you. From Lily.* Her tongue is between her teeth as she clutches the pencil.

"Lily, don't you want to play with your friends at the other centers?" I ask.

Lily shakes her head, her eyes on her pink sandals.

"What's up, buddy? You look sad."

"You know how Chloe's birthday party is this weekend?"

"Yes," I say. "It's going to be fun!" Chloe's mom has hired me to be a

64

birthday-party assistant, so I'll be there too. I didn't see this job coming at all. That makes it extra special.

"Well, Mommy still hasn't bought the purple pony. I promised Chloe I would get her the pony with the mane that you comb and braid."

"Maybe your mom hasn't had time to go shopping yet."

Lily shakes her head. "She said I won't need a gift."

That's strange. Chloe's mom read me the guest list a few days ago. Lily's name is definitely on it.

Lily looks like her whole world hinges on getting the purple pony for Chloe. I remember about Lily's dad not paying his child support. Maybe Lily's mom can't afford a present. That's happened to me before.

I'm about to tell Lily that we can make a necklace for Chloe when her face lights up. She flies across the room with her arms outstretched. "Daddy! You're here! You're here!"

The tall man at the door smiles. His curly brown hair falls across his face as he bends to pick Lily up. "Of course I'm here."

My face burns. I feel like throwing fistfuls of sand into his eyes. How dare he say that? If he wants to spend time with Lily so badly, where was he on the weekend?

He turns toward me. "I'm Blake," he says. "You must be Simone. My little ballerina–vet has told me so much about you."

I am too furious to answer.

Thankfully, Lily speaks up. "Do you want to see the pictures me and Simone painted tonight?"

"Sure."

Lily points to the easel behind me.

"Hey, you're both wearing your green necklaces!"

"Yes! Take my picture in front of it, Daddy!"

I notice that Blake has a camera case hanging from his shoulder.

"Daddy takes really good pictures, Simone," Lily says. "Come into the picture with me."

"That's okay," I say. "You go ahead."

But Lily insists. While Blake adjusts the settings, I try to unclench my jaw.

Blake doesn't take the picture right away. I'm sure he's waiting for me to smile. Eventually he snaps a few, then puts his camera away.

"Why don't you show me what else you've been doing tonight?"

Lily takes her dad's hand and shows him around the room. I pretend to organize the books at the reading center. I slam the books onto the table. I imagine myself whacking Blake upside the head with each one.

"Do you need any help, Simone?"

I had forgotten all about Fiona. "No. I'm fine. Just fine."

"Sorry. I was only asking."

Rachel walks into the room a few minutes later. She turns pale, and her smile freezes when her eyes land on Blake.

When Lily sees her mom's face, she shies away from Blake. She comes to me and leans heavily against my legs.

Blake turns toward Rachel. "I'm glad I made it here tonight. My newsletters somehow got diverted. It's good I checked the school's online message board."

Rachel shakes her head and turns her back on him. I don't blame her.

Thank goodness Blake soon leaves. Rachel stays in the room for the next half hour. I wonder if she is waiting to see that Blake has really left.

"Lily, I need to go talk to your teacher again in the library," Rachel says.

"Okay. I'll stay here with Simone."

We are playing in the tent when Rachel returns to the classroom minutes later.

"Mommy, can't I play some more with—"

She sees the thundercloud expression on her mom's face and stops talking. At that moment, the principal comes over the PA system. He announces that Curriculum Night is officially over, and he thanks everyone for coming.

"You'd better get going," I tell Lily. "I need to clean up in here."

"Okay!" Lily gives me a hug, then follows her mom out the door.

Chapter Nine

Mom beams as I get ready for Chloe's birthday party on Sunday. She makes a big deal about me getting this job all by myself.

I glance at the clock. "Gotta run!"

When I get to Chloe's house, I hang up some pony decorations. I also set out the party hats and plates and napkins. Chloe is dancing with excitement. I paint her fingernails, and she introduces me to all of her stuffed toys. Her cake is supposed to be a surprise, but I let her peek into the box.

Her friends start to arrive. Every time the doorbell rings, I expect to hear Lily's voice. But twenty minutes later, Lily is the only guest who is not here. Chloe's mom looks nervously at her watch. With the living room full of bouncy kindergarten kids, she can't hold off any longer. I listen for Lily as I lead the kids in a game of pass-the-parcel.

When everyone has a toy to play with, I slip into the kitchen to phone Lily. It sounds like somebody picks up the phone on the second ring. Then the phone goes dead.

"Simone," Chloe's mom says as she steps into the kitchen, "the kids want you to play hide-and-seek."

They cheer as I step back into the room.

"Come hide with me, Simone," Grace says.

"No, with me," Yvette says.

"You guys all hide," I say. "I'll find you instead."

As I count to twenty, I wonder again about Lily. Where is she? And why can't Rachel afford a birthday gift? She can afford dozens of pink outfits for Lily.

I try to focus and do a good job. But thoughts of Lily keep creeping back in. As Mimi giggles from behind the television, I remember Lily telling me that she doesn't have a television anymore. The week before that, she said her computer was gone.

"They weren't even broken," Lily had said. "But Mommy didn't answer me when I asked about them."

Once again, I realize that I am not doing my job.

"Come on." Mimi tucks her hand into mine. "I can help you find the others."

We head into the laundry room. I see someone wiggling underneath a bath towel in the laundry hamper.

"I see you!" Mimi pulls the towel off of Hannah. The two little girls squeal with laughter.

Some boxes rustle at the far end of the laundry room. I stand back as Mimi and Hannah rush in and find Chloe and Justine.

The little girls lead me upstairs to Chloe's purple bedroom. I stand in the middle while they check under the bed. I try to pay attention to the game. But still, Hannah has to remind me that we've found everyone.

"Yippee! Time for presents!" Chloe calls out as we storm down the stairs behind her. "Presents next, right, Mommy?"

Chloe is soon ripping into her gifts. The mound of stuffed puppies and ponies, packages of markers, lip-gloss sets and books is growing at her feet.

Chloe's mom motions to get my attention. "Simone, can you pour the juice?"

"Sure." I step into the kitchen.

One of the moms is pouring a cup of coffee by the table. She turns and smiles. "Hi. I'm Tara, Justine's mom. You must be Simone. I have heard so much about you."

"P-pardon?" It feels like her words just grabbed me by the throat.

"I said I'm Tara. And that I have heard so much about you."

I have heard so much about you.

That was it!

Tara is staring at me. I force myself to keep pouring the juice even though my hands are shaking.

I have heard so much about you.

What is it about those words? When did I last hear them?

I am passing plates of cake around when it hits me. Blake said those same words at Curriculum Night. But that makes no sense. Absolutely none.

Rachel said that Blake had had no contact with Lily since last July. But at Curriculum Night, he knew my name, and he knew about the ballerina–vet picture. He also knew about our matching green necklaces. How could that be if Lily hadn't talked to her dad for three months?

My stomach bottoms out on me. It feels like something is terribly wrong with Lily. I need to go check on her.

As I am bolting for the kitchen door, I realize I'm holding a plate with birthday cake. I pause long enough to set it on the counter.

"Are you okay?" Chloe's mom says.

I mutter something about not feeling well. Then I brush past the moms and sprint for home. Minutes later, I fly through our front door.

"Mom! Mom!"

There's no answer. Then I see the note on the counter.

Got called to work. Not sure when I'll be home. Mom xo

My heart sinks. All I know is I have to see Lily.

The bike. I'll bike over. I race to the garage and grab it. As I push it outside, I notice that the tires are completely flat. I drop the bike onto its side and race back into the house.

I pace around the kitchen, trying to figure out what to do. If something is up at Lily's house, I'd better have someone there with me. But I don't have a single friend to call.

Then an idea hits me. I can't think about it for long, or I'll chicken out. I grab the phone and dial.

I can barely hear Aaron's voice over the sound of little boys asking, "Is this one of your girlfriends again?"

I don't have time to blush. "Aaron, it's Simone. I can't talk now, but I need you to do something for me."

"Simone? What's up?"

"I think something's wrong at Lily's house."

"O-kaay." Aaron pauses.

"I know this sounds weird, but we need to go check."

"Sure. Um, don't you live pretty far away though?"

"Sort of." I don't want to think about how long it will take me to run there.

"Which way will you be coming from?" Aaron asks.

"Seventy-Sixth Avenue."

"Okay. I'll meet you along Seventy-Sixth."

Moments later, I am tearing off down the road.

Chapter Ten

I run until a stitch jabs into my side. As I turn onto 76th Avenue, I slow to a walk. My breath is coming in gasps. I don't see Aaron until he is right in front of me.

"Here." He hands me a helmet. "Climb onto the handlebars. I'll double you the rest of the way."

The helmet doesn't fit well, and getting onto the handlebars is way tougher than it sounds.

"Ouf!" I land against Aaron's chest as he starts pedaling. Our heads bang against each other. If we weren't wearing helmets, we would probably both have concussions.

Aaron is soon puffing hard. There are two more quick turns before Lily's house. At the first turn, I nearly slide off. Aaron struggles to keep the bike balanced. As he slows down for the last turn, I jump off and start running.

Lily's house is just ahead. I'm about to run up the driveway when Blake appears from around the side of the house. That must be his car parked on the street. I skid to a stop, and Aaron nearly plows into the back of me.

"Quick!" I motion to Aaron, and we run behind the garden shed next door. We watch Blake through the bushes.

Blake is so busy peering in the windows and knocking on the door that he doesn't notice us. He checks his watch, then disappears around the side of the house again. He soon appears at the other side. Neither Aaron nor I move a muscle as he rings the doorbell again and again. Then he stomps back to his car. The whole time, he is muttering to himself.

We wait until Blake has driven away before we come out from behind the shed.

"Who was that?" Aaron says.

"Blake. Lily's dad."

Aaron notices the sourness in my voice. "Oh. So you don't like him much?"

I tell Aaron about Blake missing his support payments and not showing up for his visits with Lily.

"Rachel doesn't even give out their real address because of him," I say.

"Then how did he find out Lily lives here?" Aaron asks.

I hadn't thought of that! My breath catches in my throat.

"I don't know." I shake my head. "Somehow he seems to know everything."

I fill Aaron in on Curriculum Night and how Blake knew a bunch of stuff about Lily and me that he shouldn't have known.

"That's pretty creepy," Aaron says. "What do we do now?"

"I don't know. Something still doesn't feel right to me. But now that he's gone, I guess we should go home."

As we walk down the street, I tell Aaron about Lily missing the birthday party. Then a car drives past us, and I jump.

"Oh, I thought that was Blake coming back," I say. "You know, I have no idea what that guy is up to, but I don't trust him one bit."

That night, Mom goes to bed right after dinner. She has another early start at work tomorrow. I can tell these wonky hours at the deli are hard on her.

As usual, this house feels bigger and quieter than what I'm used to. I log on to Facebook. Once again, there are no messages waiting for me. I tell myself that I should stop checking. It is too depressing. I read a few of the posts, but they are just as depressing. Most of them are about band trips and team tryouts that don't include me.

I log off the computer and turn on the TV instead. I flip through the channels. A couple with six kids wins a massive dream home. Prizewinning cupcakes are decorated like superheroes. Last but not least, a disgraced cheerleader has to dress up in a chicken costume as the school mascot at the next football game.

I am about to turn off the TV when a news update comes on. I look at the reporter's fresh makeup, perfect teeth, stylish hair and tailored suit. I wonder why they all look the same. I shake my head.

"In local news today," says the reporter, "a mother and her young daughter are believed to have been abducted from their south Edmonton home. Talia Myers reports live from the scene."

The camera moves from the newsroom to outdoors. Yep, more perfect hair and teeth.

"Earlier today, a neighbor noticed the shattered front window and the open door at this south Edmonton home. He alerted the police, who arrived to find the home ransacked. More upsetting yet—the occupants, a single mother and her five-year-old daughter, are missing.

"The woman's ex-husband, who is also the father of the young girl, is currently being questioned by police. The man was seen on the premises earlier today. He is believed to be the prime suspect in this apparent double abduction."

The reporter goes on to say the usual stuff. Names being withheld. Whereabouts unknown. Police requesting the public's assistance.

The camera pans across the front yard. I can see the whole house. It is surrounded by yellow police tape.

Something about the house looks familiar. My stomach tightens into a hard knot.

No, I tell myself. It can't be!

The camera swings farther to the right. Now I can see the neighbor's garden shed.

Oh no! It's the same shed Aaron and I hid behind earlier.

It's Lily's house! Lily must be the little girl who was abducted!

I race to the foot of the stairs. "Mom! *Mom*!"

I blurt out how Lily missed the party and about my going over to her house because I thought something was wrong. I finish by telling Mom about the news report.

Minutes later, Mom and I bolt out the door.

Chapter Eleven

The two police officers behind the counter are chatting about last night's hockey game. I wait for a moment. Then I interrupt them.

"I was there today," I say.

"I beg your pardon?"

"I was there today. At that house where the little girl was abducted."

I'm talking way louder than usual, even with both officers looking at me. "I saw the news clip on TV," I say. "It's the same house. I know because I was hiding behind the garden shed at the neighbor's house. I was watching."

"Watching what?"

I'm opening my mouth to tell him when he raises his hand. "Wait a minute." He points at Mom. "Who is this?"

"My mom."

He nods. "I'd like both of you to step into the back."

He leads us down a hallway to a small room. With its wooden table and straight-backed chairs, it looks almost like a study room at the library.

"Someone will be with you in a moment."

The same constable returns with a second officer.

"I'm Constable Dakin," she says.

I can't help but stare at her. She is smaller than me, and she looks more like a ballet dancer than a police officer.

I peel my eyes away. I need to focus, but my mind isn't doing so great at that. So before Constable Dakin asks me anything, I start talking about what happened. I tell her everything I can remember. I start from when Aaron and I arrived at Lily's house.

Constable Dakin keeps asking me to tell parts of it over again.

"You were at Lily's house with your friend?"

I pause. I don't know how to answer that. Is Aaron actually a friend? I'll have to think about that later.

"I was there with a guy from school," I say. "His name is Aaron McGavin. I don't know his exact address, but I could show you where he lives. I know his cell number too."

Out of the corner of my eye, I watch Mom's eyes growing. During the short bus ride to the police station, I had told her about Lily's family. I didn't mention anything about Aaron. I'll probably have some explaining to do when we get home.

Constable Dakin takes down Aaron's cell number. Then she asks me to back up to when I first met Lily and her family. I tell her about the Kinderbuddy project. I also tell her about meeting Blake at Curriculum Night.

"So that's how I knew it was him at Lily's house," I say.

She asks me what Blake was wearing earlier today. She asks me to describe the car he drove away in too. My heart races as I try to remember the details.

"Did the house look disturbed in any way?" Constable Dakin asks.

"No. It just looked like nobody was home."

"Why do you say that?"

"Because Blake knocked on the front door. He rang the doorbell three or four times. Nobody answered. He looked in all the windows too."

"So nothing about the house looked amiss?"

I'm about to ask Constable Dakin what she means when I remember something. The TV reporter mentioned a shattered window and an open door. "The house was fine," I say. "The windows weren't broken, and the door was closed."

Meanwhile, I'm starting to squirm on my chair. I've answered the questions as best I can. But nobody has told me the most important thing of all. I can't wait any longer.

"Do you know where Lily is?"

Constable Dakin gives me a sad look. "At this point, no. We don't know where Lily or her mother are."

My heart slams into the back of the chair. My eyes fill with tears. I wipe them away with my sleeve.

"But it said on the news that you talked to Blake. He's not a good dad to Lily. He was mean to Rachel too. And why was he sneaking around their house?"

Mom puts her hand on my arm. I know she wants me to stop saying these things. But I need to say them. The police need to know.

"We've been talking to Lily's father," Constable Dakin says. "Believe me, Simone, we're taking this very seriously.

"You're right to be upset. But we are going to assume that Lily is all right and that we'll find her. We're doing everything we can. And you've been very helpful."

I clamp my mouth shut. I don't feel like I was helpful. If it hadn't taken me until the birthday party to figure out something was going on with Lily's family, maybe she'd be safe at home right now.

Chapter Twelve

That night, the words *abducted, where-abouts unknown* and *ransacked* play out in my head. Every time I doze off, I'm thrown into a nightmare. In one, I'm watching Lily get taken from her house. In another, the stack of pictures she has drawn for me is blowing away in a gust of wind. And worst of all, I can hear her saying the words she always wrote at the bottom of the pictures she gave me. *Hi Simone. I love you. From Lily.*

It's late when I finally drop into a deep sleep. I don't hear my alarm when it goes off. Mom isn't there to wake me because she's at work.

When I finally wake up, it's after ten o'clock. I scramble to get ready for school. Period two is nearly over when I arrive. Instead of going to the junior-high wing, I circle around to the kindergarten classroom. I pull myself up onto a ledge to peer inside the window.

The kindergarten students are sitting on the carpet, singing. They are holding little bells and drums. Yuri is whacking his drum against his head. The little friends from Chloe's birthday party are sitting together. I zone in on that group especially. But, like I expect, Lily is not there.

I shift to the left. From here, I see that her cubbyhole by the classroom door is empty. My heart sinks into my sneakers, and I'm shaking all over. I had hoped that this nightmare would be over by morning.

I'm turning to leave when someone blows a whistle behind me. I nearly jump out of my shoes. I slip off the ledge I've been perched on. I skin my knuckles against the bricks on the way down.

"I don't even want to know why you're peeking into that window instead of going to class. Just get there. Now!" The outdoor ed teacher, arms loaded with stopwatches and compasses, glares at me.

I circle around to the junior-high wing. I can feel the teacher's eyes burning holes into my back the whole way.

At the office, the secretary asks why I am late.

You don't really want me to answer that.

"I slept in," I say.

She lets out her breath in a loud huff. "That's hardly an acceptable excuse. But since you're not a chronic offender…"

Her voice trails off. She signs a late slip and shoves it across the desk at me.

I slip into English class quietly. Or rather, I try to.

"Nice hair," Tessa laughs. Her hair, of course, is pulled back in a perfect ponytail. A cute hair band holds it in place.

I try to remember whether I combed my hair this morning or not. I think not. With all the tossing and turning I did last night, it's probably sticking out everywhere. I reach up and try to smooth it down. The Runway Girls break into peals of laughter.

When she can finally speak again, Stacy pipes up. "She probably slept in that T-shirt last night too."

I glance down at my shirt. It wasn't one of my better finds at the thrift store.

And given how fast I dressed this morning, I think I *did* sleep in it.

Mr. Gibson is working with a small group at the other side of the room. He looks up. "Girls, keep it down over there. Simone, the handout is on my desk. Go grab a copy and get to work, please."

The Runway Girls nudge each other and giggle as I make my way up the aisle. Apparently, they're enjoying checking out my hair and my T-shirt from the rear view too. I wish they would fall off the face of the Earth. My head is buzzing with worry about Lily. I know one thing only. I can't take much more of this.

The day doesn't improve. So I don't know whether to feel relieved or worried when I get called to the office after lunch.

I sit in one of those straight-backed chairs that are like torture devices. Minutes later, Aaron arrives.

"You got called down too?"

"Yeah." Aaron looks sleepy and untidy. For some reason, it looks cute on him. I bet the Runway Girls didn't snicker when they saw him today.

Aaron yawns. "The police came by last night to ask questions about Lily. I couldn't sleep after that."

"I didn't sleep either. I saw a news report last night. I knew it was Lily's house. Mom took me to the police, and I told them about seeing Blake. I gave them your name." I pause and take a deep breath. "Sorry I didn't get the chance to let you know."

"That's okay." He smiles and runs his hand through his hair.

"Even still—"

That's as far as I get before Ms. Boyd steps into the waiting area.

"I understand you two had an eventful day yesterday," she says.

We open our mouths to speak. But apparently Ms. Boyd isn't expecting an answer. She motions us toward a back office.

"I understand you both spoke with the police last night about Lily's disappearance. An officer named—" She checks her notes. "Constable Dakin phoned today. She might need to ask you some follow-up questions in the next few days.

"I phoned your parents. Both of your mothers have limited availability. They have given me permission to be the adult present should the police wish to ask you more questions.

"I have asked that they make as little impact as possible. Constable Dakin has assured me that she will drive an unmarked police car should she need to come to the school. She will also dress in plain clothes instead of her uniform.

And I want you both to know that I will be with you at all times."

We are probably supposed to be reassured by those last words. Somehow, they feel more like a threat. I knew Ms. Boyd was hardly the warm-fuzzies type. But jeez, she might at least ask us how we're doing. I keep my eyes on the floor.

"Aaron, you may go now. I need a few minutes with Simone."

Oh no! My heart hammers in my chest. What is Ms. Boyd going to say next?

Before she has a chance to say anything, I jump in with a question. "Have they arrested Blake yet?"

Ms. Boyd slowly removes her glasses. She takes a deep breath. "I don't know. In fact, they told me virtu-ally nothing. It occurs to me, though, that you may need extra support in the days ahead."

"You mean until Lily is safe at home and Blake is arrested?"

Ms. Boyd takes a long look at me. "Until Lily is found." She pauses. "And until then, what can I do to help you?"

My chin drops to my chest. I finally lift my head and look at Ms. Boyd.

"Nothing," I say. "There's nothing you can do."

I close the door quietly behind me as I walk out of her office.

Chapter Thirteen

It's nearly the end of the week, and the police have not shown up to talk to Aaron or me. I'm in no hurry to talk to them, but it might seem like something was happening if I did. I feel like the police aren't making any progress at all.

In the meantime, school has become even more unbearable. There has been a lot in the news about Lily's abduction.

People who have never talked to me before keep trying to chat with me about what happened. Also, the Runway Girls have noticed a connection between Aaron and me. I've become interesting to them as a result. I preferred it when they ignored me or snickered at my bad hair.

To top everything off, this is a Kinderbuddy day in leadership class. We are supposed to start organizing the Halloween party today. As we step into the elementary-wing hallway, Lily's friends wave at me. They must have asked their teacher why Lily is away. I wonder what Mrs. Mankowski told them.

I break into a burning-hot sweat. A wave of dizziness hits me next. I can't do this!

I turn and stumble down the hall. I'm standing by my locker, shaking, when Ms. Boyd finds me. "You can go back to my classroom if you'd like, Simone."

I stagger back to her classroom. I flop onto a chair and drop my head into my hands. I don't know how long I sit like that.

"You okay?" It's Aaron's voice.

"I guess. It's just—"

"Yeah. I know," he says.

I don't feel like talking, and I've just noticed there are tears pouring down my face. But there's something I need to say. "Aaron, I'm really sorry."

"Sorry?"

I take a deep breath. "For pulling you into this. If I hadn't done that, everything would still be okay for you. You wouldn't have had a police car at your house. And you wouldn't be waiting for the police to come by with more questions."

"Yeah, except that Lily is still gone. I care about what happens to her too, you know."

"Sorry. Yeah. I just meant—"

I realize it was better when I wasn't saying anything. When the bell rings, we both pick up our stuff and shuffle out the door.

I'm so dazed from not sleeping and from worrying that I hardly realize I'm actually following through on my plan. I'm becoming an expert at making posters in leadership class.

Ms. Boyd hasn't softened much since Lily was abducted, but she understands that I can't go to the kindergarten class with Lily still missing. On Kinderbuddy days, I stay in Ms. Boyd's classroom and make posters.

The posters are starting to run together in my mind. Bake sales. Pizza days. Anti-bullying. Drama club. Aaron often works with me. I think he also has a hard time going to the kindergarten class.

Fiona must have asked to stay too, because she joins us most days.

I have a hard time pulling my mind away from Lily, but I've always liked doing art. And Fiona is really good at it. She brings felt-tip markers in all colors and thicknesses, acrylic paint and paintbrushes, glitter glue and calligraphy pens. They make our posters stand out really well. Even Ms. Boyd seems impressed.

It's the end of class, and the rest of the kids have returned from the kindergarten room. I'm packing up the supplies with Fiona when Ms. Boyd calls Aaron and me to the side of the room. The Runway Girls have mostly lost interest in me again, but they perk up when Ms. Boyd says Aaron's name.

"The secretary called me from the office," Ms. Boyd says. "The police have further questions for you two. Constable Dakin is waiting for us."

As we make our way to the office, my stomach is flip-flopping. Beads of sweat form on my forehead and upper lip. A trickle runs down the middle of my back.

What if they have news about Lily? And what if the news isn't good? My throat tightens, and I nearly choke.

"You'll need to wait here, Aaron," Ms. Boyd says. "Constable Dakin wants to talk to Simone first."

I'm not sure I'm ready for this. I glance at Aaron. He looks way calmer than me. Or maybe he's also terrified but can hide it better than I can.

Constable Dakin is not wearing her uniform. That makes her look even less like a police officer.

Ms. Boyd plunks down into the chair beside me in the assistant principal's office.

"Constable Dakin," she begins, "I have the families' permission to be the adult present with my students. Neither Simone nor Aaron's parents are available."

"But Simone and Aaron aren't being charged with anything."

"Well, no," Ms. Boyd stammers. "Of course not, but—"

"They don't need an adult present on their behalf."

"Oh."

I glance at Ms. Boyd. Her mouth is open, but no words are coming out. For once, she is speechless. If I wasn't so scared, I would laugh out loud.

Instead, I say something that surprises even me. "Actually, I'd like Ms. Boyd to stay."

I wonder how much I'll be allowed to ask. Will the police tell me any official information?

I'm about to test it out when Constable Dakin says, "Just so you know, we have not yet found Lily or Ms. Warnicke."

Oh no—Rachel! My mind has been so filled with thoughts of Lily that I've hardly thought about Rachel at all. I feel a twinge of guilt. Then images of Lily crowd back in.

"I need to ask you a few questions about Ms. Warnicke," Constable Dakin says. "Had she said anything to you about going anywhere? Moving, or going on a trip maybe?"

That wasn't what I expected. I shake my head.

Constable Dakin looks like she is going to move on to the next question. Then I remember something.

"Actually Lily said something about a new house. One with dolphins and a swing set and sandcastles."

I realize how silly that must sound. Constable Dakin likely thinks I'm just a dumb kid. "I don't know if that counts though."

"You never know," Constable Dakin says.

She is probably humoring me. Why isn't she asking about Blake? It's like she's forgotten all about him.

"Were you ever inside Lily's house?"

"No. I stopped there one day to return something. But I didn't go inside."

"Why was that?"

"Rachel was outside when I got there. Lily wanted me to go inside with her. Then Rachel called me back outdoors."

"When did this happen?"

"Um, it was the weekend before Curriculum Night. On the Saturday afternoon."

"When was Curriculum Night?"

I glance sideways at Ms. Boyd. "It was October thirteenth," she says. "That was a Wednesday evening."

"So the previous Saturday was—" Constable Dakin flips through her notebook "—October ninth." She writes, then looks back up at me. "Did you see anything inside the house?"

"All I saw was some boxes inside the front door. They had clothes spilling out of them."

"Did you notice anything about them?"

"I'm pretty sure they were Lily's. They were pink. Her mom buys her a lot of pink clothes."

As Constable Dakin writes this down, I wait for her to ask me about Blake.

"Did Lily mention anything out of the ordinary going on at her house?"

"Not really. But Rachel told me that Blake missed a lot of his scheduled visits with Lily."

Constable Dakin hardly seems interested. "What about at her actual house—with her mom?"

I can't believe she keeps pulling the conversation away from Blake.

I rack my brain. "It's hard. Lily jumps from one idea to the next when she talks. But she said the TV and computer disappeared. Rachel wouldn't tell her why when she asked. According to Lily, neither one was broken."

Constable Dakin writes this down.

Seriously? She's more interested in the TV and the computer than in Blake?

"Did you ever notice anything unusual about Rachel's behavior?"

"Well, yeah. She was moody. It was hard to figure out if she was happy or friendly or not."

It feels awful talking this way about Rachel, considering she got abducted too. She's also in danger. Yet I've hardly given her a thought.

"I don't blame Rachel though," I say quickly. "Blake made her life really tough."

There. Hopefully I've got this interview back on track.

"Can you think of any other unusual situations with Rachel?"

I grit my teeth before I answer. "The first day we started the Kinderbuddy project, Rachel came into the kindergarten class. She was checking if Lily was okay."

"And was she okay?"

"Lily was sad at first because she was supposed to work with a boy. She was afraid of Aaron in the beginning."

"Okay, so Lily was upset. Had the teacher phoned Rachel to come into the classroom as a result?"

"I don't think so." I glance at Ms. Boyd.

She clears her throat. "Mrs. Mankowski and I worked together for the entire class. I can confirm that Mrs. Mankowski did not phone Lily's mother. There was no need. The child was momentarily upset. Then she settled down."

"I worked with Lily for the rest of the class," I say. "Lily was great. We had a fun time together."

A huge lump pushes its way up into my throat.

Constable Dakin is still writing. She doesn't even look back up at me. "Thank you, Simone. I'd like to speak with Aaron now."

As I leave the office, every muscle in my body is clenched. It seems Lily has just vanished. But that can't be. And why didn't Constable Dakin want to know a single thing about Blake?

I am all the way down the hall before something occurs to me.

Maybe Blake didn't abduct Lily and Rachel after all.

Chapter Fourteen

That night, I'm too restless to sleep. Mom's not going to be home from work for a while. I've been rattling around the house by myself for too long. I don't feel like going to bed yet, so I pull a chair up in front of the computer. I try to brace myself for disappointment as I log on to Facebook.

But what's this? I can't believe it. I actually have a message. Lauren or Danielle must have messaged me after all.

Hang on a second. It's from—who? Teresita Romero? I've never heard of her. She's probably writing to tell me about the million dollars I won in some fake lottery overseas. I slump down in the chair as my eye scrolls over the message.

Hello. I help the mother here. I babysit little girl.

She say you are best friend.

She miss you.

She want I tell you, Hi Simone. I love you. From Lily.

That familiar message that I thought I'd never see again! My mind is zipping in a hundred different directions. Every muscle in my body is twitching as I read the message again.

It sounds like Lily is safe. And she's somewhere with her mother?

Just who are you, Teresita? And where do you live?

As I click on her name, I pray she's not the cautious type. I hope she has lots of information on her Facebook page.

She has an open profile. I learn that she is employed at Jubilation Hotel and Resort. She lives in Puerto Vallarta, Mexico.

So Lily is in Mexico?

I don't even breathe until I have Constable Dakin on the phone.

After believing for so long that Blake abducted Lily, it's hard to shift my thinking. I feel awful for the things I've thought and said about Blake. So at first I don't know what to do when Constable Dakin phones me to talk about him.

"Blake would like to speak with you, Simone. He asked me to give you his phone number. He'd like you to call him, if that's possible."

"Why?"

"I understand he would like to thank you," Constable Dakin says.

"For what?"

"For being a good friend to Lily. For being the person she knew she could reach out to. She didn't try contacting anyone else, you know."

I can't stop the tears at this point. But when they finally let up, I dial Blake's number.

"Hello, Blake? It's Simone."

"Simone, I'm so glad you phoned. I've been hoping to thank you for—"

"No," I say. "Please don't thank me. I thought some horrible things about you. I was wrong, and I'm really sorry."

"You don't have to be sorry. Rachel had a good smear campaign going against me. I don't blame you for believing all the things you heard. Of course people thought the worst of me.

"As for Lily, the police located her quickly after you gave them Teresita's Facebook information. I'm flying to Puerto Vallarta first thing tomorrow morning to be with Lily. We fly home on Monday."

"Is, uh, Rachel flying home too?"

"Actually, no. She hasn't returned since the police found Lily at the hotel with Teresita. They haven't apprehended Rachel yet."

"But Lily is okay?"

"Yes. I talked to her earlier. She knows I'm coming to bring her home. She's pretty confused—especially with her mother having disappeared. But it's okay. We know she's safe." His voice cracks. I hear the sincerity in it. I feel horrible all over again for thinking he was the bad parent.

"By the way," Blake says, "I wonder if you could do me a favor. Could you meet us at the airport when we arrive home? I think it would really help Lily to see you."

I think about all the news stories and the photos and the TV reports that I have tried to ignore since Lily vanished. I picture swarms of reporters at the airport.

"Will I really get to see her?" I ask. "I mean, won't lots of reporters and other people be there too?"

"Hopefully not. I'm trying to keep our return date from the media. I haven't told anyone else. Lily has been traumatized enough. Please promise me you won't tell anyone. Other than your mother, of course."

As I write down the flight information, I wonder how I'll get to the airport Friday night. It's way south of the city, and Mom doesn't have a car. She's probably working anyway. I have to get there somehow.

"I'll be there for sure," I say. "I'll see you and Lily then."

The three days before Lily flies home drag on forever. Mom has to work most of the weekend, but she tries to find diversions for me. We bake cookies, and we go online to figure out how I'll get to the airport. It looks like the airport shuttle bus is the best option. Mom insists on giving me the money for it.

When Friday finally comes, I can hardly concentrate at school. The minute classes end, I race home. I have checked and double-checked the bus schedule, but I pull it up again on the computer.

I don't have to catch the shuttle bus until 6:45 PM. I'm so worried about missing it, or about the bus being delayed, that I catch the 5:45 bus instead. That means I have to wait a long time at the airport before Lily's flight arrives. I try to peel my eyes away from the clocks, but I can't. To add to everything, Lily's flight is delayed by forty minutes.

By the time Lily walks through the gate, holding Blake's hand, I am shaking with emotion. My heart inflates like a massive hot-air balloon as Lily turns and sees me. Blake smiles as Lily launches herself into my arms. She hugs me tightly and says my name over and over. I can't say anything for a while.

Chapter Fifteen

I spend a lot of time with Blake and Lily after they get home. In talking with Blake, I learn that he knew Lily's real address all along. She gave it to him months before she got confused by the fake address I taught her in class.

I also learn that Rachel sold off her valuables and emptied out her bank accounts. The police think she ransacked her own house before she took Lily away. All of this was to keep Blake from seeing their daughter again—and to get him convicted for the crime she committed—parental child abduction.

Now that Lily lives with him full time, Blake says he needs a steadier income than what he earns as a freelance photographer. His trip to Mexico to get Lily was expensive too. He'll soon start working in a camera shop.

I get a new job too. Blake hires me to babysit Lily after school. Mom is beaming when I tell her. "So what are you going to do with the money you earn?" Mom asks.

The question catches me by surprise. I don't want to look like a Runway Girl. But it might be nice to buy clothes that somebody else didn't wear first. I might change my mind about that, but I would like to see for myself.

With Lily home safely, it feels like a happy ending. But she is sad, too. She often asks where her mommy is and when she is coming home. It's hard for Lily to understand that nobody knows.

One day Lily tells me she is also sad that she missed the Halloween party the Kinderbuddies and the Big Buddies planned together.

"Was it fun, Simone?"

"I don't know. I didn't go."

I had stayed by myself in Ms. Boyd's class that day while Fiona and Aaron went with their Kinderbuddies.

"You missed it too?" Lily asks.

"Of course. I didn't want to go without you."

"Were you sad you missed it?"

I don't know what to say. I was sad that day, but only because I was so worried about Lily.

I look at her and nod. "Yes, I was sad too."

Then I get a great idea. "You know," I say, "we could plan our own Halloween party."

Lily stands up straighter. "But don't we have to wait until *next* Halloween?"

"No." I shake my head. "We can have our Halloween party whenever we want."

Lily is starting to bounce. "Can we have it at the playground tomorrow?"

I laugh. "It might be better if we wait until the weekend. That will give us time to buy some candy and prizes."

Lily's eyes grow. "And can we wear costumes?"

"Yes."

"And can we invite our friends?"

"We can definitely invite our friends."

I smile. It's a huge change for me to realize that I have real friends at school now. Aaron and Lily. And I've started to spend time with Fiona too. I don't know why I ever thought she was dying to become a Runway Girl. I sure had that wrong.

We worked together through lunch a few times while we were decorating posters. Now we eat lunch together every day in the cafeteria. And every day after school, Fiona comes with me when I go pick up Lily. Then we stop at the grade-one class while Fiona picks up Olivia, her little sister. Lily was jealous of Olivia in the beginning, but now she likes her. The four of us spend hours at the playground together. Aaron and his brothers sometimes show up too. Reilly, Dexter and Carson are even wilder than Yuri.

That week, Lily and I shop for candy and toys. Blake paid me last week, and all of the leftover Halloween stuff is on sale in the stores.

On Friday, Lily and I bake cupcakes. I want to set them aside to cool, but Lily can't wait to decorate them. A lot of the icing runs off the hot cupcakes, but Lily doesn't seem to notice. She dumps tons of sprinkles on top and claps her hands with excitement when she has finished.

"Look, Simone. The cupcakes are beautiful!"

"Yes. Everyone will love them," I say.

I have all of the party supplies waiting beside the door when Blake drops Lily off on Saturday. She giggles when I pretend I don't recognize her in her costume. She is wearing a pair of black plastic-frame glasses. A long white shirt of her dad's, unbuttoned, is over her fall jacket. The shirt reaches almost to the floor. A stuffed puppy is in one pocket, and a toy kitten is in the other. She is also wearing a tutu underneath her lab coat.

"Look! I am a ballerina–vet!" Lily twirls for me. She nearly trips on her veterinary coat. "Where is your costume?"

"You have to help me put it on," I say.

I pull on Mom's red winter coat. Lily helps me stick black construction-paper dots on it. She also adjusts my head band with the two antennae. I slip a set of wings onto my back.

"Do you know what I am?" I ask.

"You are a pretty ladybug!" she says as we head out the door.

We are the first to arrive at the playground. Soon a clown and a witch show up. Lily bounces up and down as she greets Fiona and Olivia.

Aaron arrives next, wearing a yellow hard hat, a fluorescent vest and a pair of work gloves.

"Hello, Construction Worker Man!" Lily laughs.

Loud voices ring out behind Aaron. Reilly, Dexter and Carson storm onto the playground next. They are dressed as a farmer, Batman and a hockey player. Within seconds, they are wrestling in the sand and trying to pull each other off the monkey bars.

Now that everyone is here, I give Lily, Olivia and the little boys empty goody bags. Aaron, Fiona and I take a package of candy to three different corners of the playground.

"You have to yell 'trick or treat' each time," Lily says, "or the Big Buddies won't give you any candy."

Later, while the kids are eating their treats, Aaron, Fiona and I hide plastic spiders and jack-o'-lantern toys around the playground. When the younger kids have found them, we pull out the cupcakes. Everyone loves them.

It's getting cold outside, and we are all starting to shiver. Still, Lily groans when Blake arrives to pick her up. "I'm not ready to go home yet."

"We don't have to go home right now," he says. "First I need to take a picture of everyone."

It takes a long time to get everyone arranged. Reilly, Dexter and Carson are too busy bumping into each other on the way down the slide to join us. Finally, Aaron coaxes his little brothers into the pirate ship with the rest of us.

"Smile," Blake says.

"Cheese!"

"Did you take the picture yet?" Lily says.

"Yes." Blake holds out his camera. "See, right there in the little window."

I can't resist looking in the little window too.

Sure enough, there we all are. Friends. Together.

Karen Spafford-Fitz studied English Language and Literature at Queen's University. She next completed a degree in education and taught elementary and junior-high students for eight years. Two daughters and one move across the country later, Karen began creating stories for children and teenagers. *Vanish* is her second middle-grade novel. When Karen is not writing, she is often training for her next half-marathon.